MISSION
CONTAMINATION

North Yorkshire

Edited By Donna Samworth

First published in Great Britain in 2019 by:

 Young**Writers**® Est. 1991

Young Writers
Remus House
Coltsfoot Drive
Peterborough
PE2 9BF
Telephone: 01733 890066
Website: www.youngwriters.co.uk

FOREWORD

Young Writers was created in 1991 with the express purpose of promoting and encouraging creative writing. Each competition we create is tailored to the relevant age group, hopefully giving each student the inspiration and incentive to create their own piece of work, whether it's a poem, mini saga or a short story. We truly believe that seeing their work in print gives students a sense of achievement and pride in their work and themselves.

Our Survival Sagas series aimed to challenge both the young writers' creativity and their survival skills! One of the biggest challenges, aside from dodging diseased hordes and avoiding the contagion, was to create a story with a beginning, middle and end in just 100 words!

Inspired by the theme of contamination, whether from a natural mutation, a chemical attack or a man-made experiment gone wrong, their mission was to craft tales of fear and redemption, new beginnings and struggles of survival against the odds. As you will discover, these students rose to the challenge magnificently and we can declare *Mission Contamination* a success.

The mini sagas in this collection are sure to set your pulses racing and leave you wondering with each turn of the page: are these writers born survivors?

CONTENTS

June Darlow-Castleton (12) 63
Bailey Orrells (12) 64
Christina Salisbury (12) 65
Sandra Kukurowska (13) 66
Sian Nichola McDonald (13) 67
William George Baniqued- 68
Smith (13)
Emily Elizabeth Owen (13) 69
Maia Jarmany (12) 70
Alec Randall (12) 71
Ella Mai Brown (13) 72
Misty Byju 73
Sienna Leigh Cunningham (13) 74
Molly Faith Squire (12) 75
Chiela Robertson (13) 76
Louis Eastwood (13) 77
George Dickinson (12) 78
Albin Johnbosco (12) 79
Frank Denham (12) 80
Lola Cammish (12) 81
Lucy Webster (11) 82
Oskar Zoremba (13) 83
Amelia Cooper (11) 84
P Jay Flanagan (12) 85
Finlay Earnshaw (11) 86
Rebecca Strickland (12) 87
Isabelle Towse (12) 88
Bhavana Binooj (12) 89
Molly Murray (11) 90
Archie Colin Austin (11) 91
Josh Beecroft (12) 92
Corey Ormston (12) 93
Kaiden Sleightholm (12) 94

The Read School, Drax

Jamie Holdich (13) 95
Millie O'Brien (12) 96
Verity Haigh 97
Camran Cook (11) 98
Sally Featherstone (12) 99

The Wensleydale School, Leyburn

Brodie Allinson 100
Chloe Cumpstone 101
Poppy Hainsworth (13) 102
Connor Rosbotham 103
Callum Fowler 104
Maciej Nuprejczyk (13) 105
Luke Dent 106
Lucas McCulloch 107
Cleo Baker 108
Aidan James Simpson (13) 109
Riley Teasdale 110
Lucy Smith 111

Upper Wharfedale School, Threshfield

Sofia Pemartin Carrillo (12) 112
Aine Kelly (13) 113
Teddy Cook (13) 114
Elliot Ashley (12) 115
Bradley Peter Smith (13) 116
Lucas Shutt (12) 117
Abbie Marshall (15) 118
Zack Daniels (12) 119
Jessica Jane Ferridge (13) 120
Charlie Bond (14) 121
Samantha Cole (13) 122
Izzy Willis (13) 123
Zoë Holme (14) 124
Kai Asquith (13) 125
Álvaro Pemartín (11) 126
Peter Johnston (13) 127
Oscar Gamble (13) 128
Chloe Evans (13) 129
Alicia Heseltine (14) 130
Jessie Allen (11) 131
Paige Spriggs (14) 132
Ailish Kelly (13) 133
Daniel Berry 134
Harrison Donne (13) 135
Isabella Sacks Alderson (13) 136
Jorja Woollaston (13) 137

Sam Meldon (12)	138
Felicia Stenzel (11)	139
Noah Peace (12)	140
Korey Michael Hopson (13)	141
Cameron Marsden (12)	142
Amirah Jahangir (15)	143
Sabiha Ayub (12)	144
Thomas Knight (13)	145
Gethin Kerswell (15)	146
Ruby Winthrop (13)	147
Mollie Roberts (15)	148
Harry Clifford Gaskell (16)	149
Harry Peace (14)	150
Chloe Maimee Barbour (11)	151
Emma Falshaw (13)	152
Charlie Smith (14)	153
Archie Allen (13)	154
James Neill (13)	155
Jan Kucia (13)	156
Alfie Roddis	157
Isabelle Lynam (14)	158
David Elgie (14)	159

THE MINI SAGAS

Mission Contamination? No Problem...

So, I'm the daughter of an evil man who hides behind the facade of being a philanthropic billionaire. Our relationship's estranged and he's a recluse - even his business is run by my mother, who believes he's the epitome of *perfect husband*. Quite the oxymoron since tomorrow he'll release a virus, killing off 90 percent of the population. Survival will mean paying absurd amounts for the cure. I need to save the world. Except, in 649 seconds, I'll be the first to be injected with a virus that will kill in ten minutes. I have to stop Mission Contamination. No problem...

Hannah Mary Orchison (13)

Malton School, Malton

The Room

The blank walls glare back at me. White. Dazzling. I've been here for four weeks. It's all my imagination. The voices. They've told me things. Things that hurt me and my friends. They've contaminated my mind. The isolation room's meant to stop them, yet they will not leave. I'm suicidal. The voices say I'm worthless. They're correct. My family left me and I've lost everything I owned. The temptation of everyday objects being weapons is too powerful and my mind is blurred. This is the end. My life's over and, as I fall to the ground, I start remembering why.

Ella Allanson (14)
Malton School, Malton

Curiosity

Humans, we're so curious. Always so eager to discover and explore, believing it was for the better. They said going to Mars would make us immortal. If something happened on Earth, those on Mars would be unaffected. But we were idiots. We thought Mars was lifeless and barren. We were so wrong. The ice on the poles contained a frozen virus. When the first people on Mars returned, we were so overjoyed. But not for long. For they were infected. The virus went airborne, waterborne and infected cattle and food. Before long, everyone was infected. Humans, we were so curious.

Isaac Gardner (14)
Malton School, Malton

The Battle Of 1,000 Bees

Everyone heads in different directions. My vision goes blurry and my stomach feels wheezy. The sky turns a shade of grey and the buzzing gets louder and louder until the foghorn is no longer audible. I follow Mother. She's my only hope. She will lead me to refuge. Suddenly, a contaminated bee appears out of nowhere and stings her in the eye. She screams in pain and a bright light flashes. She's coming towards me, smaller, with wings. She has been contaminated. I cry and can't stop. Dear Reader, help your world before it's too late. I'm so sorry...

Lily Grace Kemp (11)
Malton School, Malton

Unbalanced Death

Miserable humans, they'll all die eventually. Their resistance is useless, their lack of life skills will be their undoing. Due to my annoyance at the human race, I created a disease. It causes an imbalance in hormones found during and after puberty. This causes most adults and teens to die. I got great satisfaction from watching the terrified faces of the children as the adults around them dropped dead. However, humans continue to annoy me. A group of idiots are trying to find a cure that doesn't exist. I'll continue to monitor their futile attempts.

Josh Moir (13)
Malton School, Malton

Operation Steel Tiger

It's been four days. We are the only survivors of the French Special Forces. On Friday, 16th June, our rescue party entered Moscow. A huge cloud of nuclear radiation mutated 80 percent of the Russian population. We were attacked. Me and four others are now in the Khimki forest. We are surrounded. I had just put down my diary when a huge wave of mutants began to rain down on us. I shouldered my rifle and fired four shots which ripped into the nearest mutant. The other COS operatives also started firing at the listless hordes. The mutants were everywhere...

Kostas Bourke (13)
Malton School, Malton

Falsity Forest

I walked into the overgrown thicket of branches, the forest I always came to. It was the ticking time bomb that was optionally open - code, already uncracked. If only. Branches twisting all over the leafy surface whilst micro-catalysts grew over rotten bark. Tree torture stood there in front of my face and I couldn't even see it. The germs were multiplying. My throat tingled and my body felt warm, my body was suffocating and my blood was thinning. The sense of dryness never left and to this day, violet shapes still appear in the clear film of my vision.

Iona Spence (13)
Malton School, Malton

Safe

Dr Jones had infected the world. I needed to find him. Were the infected waiting for me, eager to spread the disease? I waited for ages before walking to the door. I unlocked it and ran towards his office. I was fumbling for the keys. I glanced behind me and went in, whispering to myself, "Still safe."

I walked over to his chair. My whole body was trembling. Dr Jones was slumped in the chair. I thought he was dead. I took a couple of steps towards the cabinet. "Not safe!" he cried!

The infected were here. I wasn't safe!

Nadine Holmes (14)
Malton School, Malton

The Contaminators Of Malton

Malton was one of the most peaceful towns in Yorkshire! It was quite surprising to find an apocalypse of zombies had overthrown the town. It was a terrifying experience for all the residents. It all started with a disease so horrible it could transform you into a brain-eating zombie from just one touch from a contaminated soul and you would immediately transform into one of the vile beasts. Their purplish skin was lumpy and disgusting, not to mention their grisly teeth. Perhaps someone can help us? Maybe one day the contamination will be defeated?

Phoebe Milson (11)
Malton School, Malton

Battle Of The Blue Light

The human race, we are so advanced in mathematics and literacy. We have invented the most extraordinary inventions ever. But now our inventions are fighting back and we are losing the battle of the blue light. Evil has contaminated the blue light and it is everywhere. Who knew that our greatest weakness came from our own brains? Phones, TVs, computers, iPads and more. We revolve around them like the sun but if that sun explodes, we will all die. I have come from the future. This is happening! I am warning you, we all need to change. Now or never!

Isabel Preece (12)
Malton School, Malton

Worms

I'm terrified. People are dying. Everywhere. First they cough, then their ears swell, finally - death. And the crops? Dead. All of them. Every farmer, every crop is suffering. But I'm alive, everyone living on the farm is. Last night my wife rushed in. "The worms!" she cried. "They're blue and short and fat!"
We're all petrified. We've got nothing to eat. Whenever we try to eat, the veg goes all dead-like and mouldy. It's all wrong. Already our weakest are dead. Perhaps tomorrow, it'll be us.

Kirsty Noble (12)
Malton School, Malton

The Final Missile

We were dead, so were many more, more were falling. The missiles fell, they fell fast - the impenetrable fog engulfing our bodies as our souls floated away, far, far away. No one knew why it happened, not us, not them, no one. But slowly, as many souls drifted together into space, we saw the neon lights in the defensive field: 'Toxic gasses, exits will be blocked in ten!'
How did they know now? How did they let us perish like this? A cure had to be found rapidly before we were joined by more. Then the final missile fell...

Alfreda Powlesland (13)
Malton School, Malton

Mutated World

Hello, I'm Ellie. I don't have much time before they come, so let me tell you my story. The year 2213, the battle between China and America spread worldwide. America was engulfed with rage. Bomb crafters made a bomb to end the war forever. As the bomb fell, Mum locked me in the basement. The last thing she said to me was, "Find hope." Now all that's left is crumbling buildings and the groaning mutants outside the door. A mutated cat barged the door down. Find a cure... it's too late for me...

Iona Eve Scrase (12)

Malton School, Malton

Infected

The siren blared, echoing. I wondered how these deformed remnants of a human managed to stand before me. Unaware of the consequences, I swept my exposed hand over its arm, stifling a gasp as it quickly fled. My gaze widened as I detected a blistering rash on my hand. I quickly pulled off my mask as I let out a blood-curdling scream, I was infected. I rested my shaking hand against my pistol, lifting it to my temple, my finger releasing the bullet. I inhaled a lungful of toxic gas before my eyes rolled back and I fell limp.

Hannah McElwain (13)

Malton School, Malton

Infection

US President, Donald Trump XX, declared the world fit for human habitation after a 200-year wait, long enough for the radiation to leave. Me, I would be opening the door. Allowing humanity to walk the earth again. Sweating with nerves, I walked up to the metal hatch and entered the pin code. Clunks and the door swung open. I was staring straight into the eyes of a mutant. Glowing green eyes like a path to Hell. I slammed the door shut, but not before a withered black hand reached out to scratch my arm. I was infected.

Henry Wilson (13)
Malton School, Malton

Bubble

My bubble is my world. It's all I have, all I can touch, anything else will kill everyone instantly. Some may say how lucky I am to live in a place free from contamination but, in fact, I am already contaminated and forced to live in isolation like all the others who are just like me. We are seen as outcasts and, through no fault of our own, are forced into this life of solitary confinement. I am treated like a deadly disease. This is my life. This is my reality, my normal. My bubble is my world.

Beth Graham (14)
Malton School, Malton

Hungry

When she returned she was pale and sweaty; although when I asked, she assured me she was alright. She kept complaining she was hungry, yet food made her sick. And that's when I noticed the bites on her arms and neck. Now I was scared. Her throat kept making inhuman, growling noises. Her jaws snapped. My heart hammering in my chest. I reached for the door as she pounced...
I woke up outside with the door open, blood everywhere and hungry. Oh, so hungry...

Amber Methven (13)
Malton School, Malton

End Of Earth

It all started when the nuke hit the Indian Ocean in 2034. No one saw it as a major issue until the death toll in Africa in 2037. Around one million people had died due to the contaminated water. Fishing had also caused a problem as all the fish were turning up dead, floating on top of the waves. Of course, people ate them, no matter the warnings. Now here I am in a world where drinking water is like suicide, waiting for darkness to overcome my weakening state.

Jacob Wallace (13)
Malton School, Malton

Poison

Luminous, tangerine, flaming eyes. Innocent people's crimson blood cascaded over the peeling, dead, furfuraceous skin beneath the shredded rags of these killers. The synchronised, menacing tribe trudged determinedly towards me on this ebony night - their leader's growls breaking the deadly silence every two minutes. Its mouth vacated, bearing the devious talons inside. Slicing through the night, the creature's arm clenched onto my head, rooting its bony fingers through my hair. My skull was pierced with its venom; I dropped dead. Silence followed. I lay there, lifeless. My head turned sharply, I smiled as I rose, joining my new murderous family.

Sadie Yeadon (12)

Sherburn High School, Sherburn In Elmet

The Bunker

Surely, Ashville was safe, huddled together in the bunker. But with the city deserted, the stronghold would collapse when the infected came. Then the parasites would unearth them. They would catch the gokenmonths disease. All it needed was for one person to catch it, then everyone would become zombies forever! A crash was heard from above. They had arrived. The destruction only went on for minutes but then the walls surrendered. They were demolished. The zombies stumbled, tripped and blundered forward, scraping at the ground until it appeared. What would be the extinction of the human race. The hand...

Alex Taylor (12)
Sherburn High School, Sherburn In Elmet

The Infection

The last drop fell into the test tube. I picked it up, never taking my eyes off it. I raised the bubbly green substance to my mouth and gulped it down with one swallow. I felt my veins pop, my mind change. *The perfect drink,* I thought. A knock at the door stopped my thoughts.

"Come in," came from my throat amidst growls.

"Did the secret ingredient work. Doctor?"

She stepped through the door. "Doctor?"

The disease had spread. It wasn't long 'til the lab was infected and now that the drink was out, the whole world would be too...

Evie Humphreys (12)

Sherburn High School, Sherburn In Elmet

The Beginning (Of The End)

Their fingers twitched. Their eyes bloodshot, wide open in a silent scream. His wrists tied to the chair. He breathed long, raspy breaths. On the other side of the mirror, men with clipboards and men with phones watched on. The man closed his eyes and opened them again. When they opened, they had a green tint around the pupil. The man shrieked and lunged and yelled, breaking his bonds and sprinting towards the mirror until his genetically hardened skull touched the glass and it shattered. Workers and scientists fled but all that survived was the message on the phone: *Contamination*.

Fintan Wheelhouse (13)
Sherburn High School, Sherburn In Elmet

Luna

The humungous swarm of demonic creatures rose in the air, hunting. Luna, the strongest, craved the delicious blood only humans could provide. Each time they fed they made sure not to kill, but if they did they feasted on the flesh, a rare treat! Only 50 left.
When the humans disappeared their only blood source would be animals. Luna needed the strongest blood to survive, without it she'd die! She needed humans. These demonic creatures kept the humans with a supply of food so they didn't die. Humans found the food vile! Luna surveyed them, laughing hysterically as they ate.

Ollie Western (14)
Sherburn High School, Sherburn In Elmet

Apocalyptic Sunset

My tail coiled round my body in discomfort, the robust stench departing from my father's room. What was this strange smell? Instability filled my senses as I rose to my feet, ears turned to a petite thud.

My father had once told me, "Don't smash or play with my bottles, threatening toxins will be exposed and put the world at risk. I advise you to avoid this room at all costs."

A painful puncture of realisation pierced my brain. Snatching my few items, I sprinted from the room. I abandoned the house, entering the dense forest as the sun descended.

Leah Eastwood (12)
Sherburn High School, Sherburn In Elmet

Six Shots

Doctor Zenon must have the formulae in his lab. Three zombies saunter through what was once the door, Rick grabs the gun. He shoots three times, making three kills. Three shots left. The world's extinct, apart from three zombies left on Earth. Two zombies wade through the various tables and lab equipment. Rick takes two shots, perfect aim. One final zombie hobbles in, he appears to be half mutated, he explains he's the last. I hear a final bullet. Rick's dead. The final zombie keels over. I'm the last man on Earth. I turn to the door. Light floods in...

Joseph Pearson (13)
Sherburn High School, Sherburn In Elmet

It Is Back

She said it would come back. She said it would kill everyone. Nobody believed her. We are all infected and now we will be slaughtered mercilessly. Nobody will survive. This horrific massacre of the human race has been coming for a long time. Unexplained incidents of villagers disappearing and corpses appearing days later coated in red dust and with flickering eyes have been reported for as long as time can remember. Humans have destroyed the world, now we must pay. Continents are piles of corpses as the apocalyptic world dies forever. Now I do not fear death but accept it.

Anna Clifton (11)
Sherburn High School, Sherburn In Elmet

The Bunker

Day 1: I emerged from my bunker with an intelligence serum. After 10 years of genetic coding, I've got it. Now I need someone to try it on.
Day 5: I've done it, I infected someone. Let's hope it went right.
Day 13: The news has confirmed my worries, my virus has started an apocalypse of zombies.
Day 17: I'm the last person on the planet with only enough serum for one more day.
Day 18: Boss, Mission Contamination is a success. We have eliminated all life on Earth by changing that scientist's solution. Now to change the world forever.

Jake Stanley Hanson (12)
Sherburn High School, Sherburn In Elmet

The Hypnosis

Another day in hell began, it was as silent as death itself. All communication cut off from the outside; TVs, phones, computers and more, never to be used again in case the hypnosis reached us. All humans controlled, not knowing their behaviour. I hadn't left my apartment in New York since the first hypnosis takeover. I wasn't planning to leave but, eventually, resources would run out. Suddenly, the front door caved. A man walked in holding a phone. I looked straight at him. He slowly stumbled towards me. He held up the phone. It was the hypnosis! Was this it...?

Evie Johnson (12)
Sherburn High School, Sherburn In Elmet

The Collapse

The ground began to shake violently, I looked out of the bedroom window in horror as the nuclear research plant, just outside of London, collapsed. Bodies were soaring through the evening sky. As the rumblings quietened, the country fell silent, only the screams of those who survived could be heard. Their deafening screams sounded inhuman. I ran downstairs to tell my mother, she sat horrified as she watched the TV. A green mist fell over London, creeping into my home through the small cracks around the door frame, slowly filling my home. I shook violently in my chair...

Taylor Jeffries (13)
Sherburn High School, Sherburn In Elmet

Beware Of The Acid Tap!

He turned the tap on to wash his hands. The pain seared through them with the power of a thousand knives. Infected Acid. Thirty minutes ago; carefree; he and Mikey entered the old hospital after hearing the scream. They searched the dark passages, scared, excited, not sure what to expect. Sam found himself outside a toilet. He went inside, he could see only by the slit in the boarded window. The metal screeched. The burning rash on his hands spread quickly over his whole body, he reached out and touched Mikey. The killer plague had begun... Could it be stopped?

Lola Ewart (12)
Sherburn High School, Sherburn In Elmet

The Humans

The tangy orange sun rose over the desolate horizon. The time had come, this one raid would prevent starvation, dehydration and disease. The worn-down chemist was 10 miles away and without a car, they would have to walk. The moaning and wailing told them that it was now or never. The group of five swiftly made their way through the old and run-down town. The five reached the chemist and started looting. It was silent. Too silent. Glass shattered from all directions with muffled cackles in the distance. This was it. The humans had found them. Everything died.

Seth Gardner (12)
Sherburn High School, Sherburn In Elmet

Excrutiating Pain

I never thought it was going to end this way. I never knew such a terrible fate could come to someone as innocent as a child. It started as a small chemical spill. It was cleaned up and nobody thought anything of it.

But then the bodies started piling up. At first it was just a subtle increase of deaths. Then they were all gone. All except The Seven. The Seven Children. As the sickening stench of stale blood drifted around the streets. It happened. The Seven Children, who at first were unaffected, began to suffer.

The pain was excruciating.

Elizabeth Sheehan (12)
Sherburn High School, Sherburn In Elmet

The Creatures

They wandered towards us, their mouths gaping and their faces dull and bruised. I was afraid and unarmed, utterly defenceless. We were bitterly cold, stood out in the open, hunting for scraps. We were clearly targets. The creatures came closer, I shut my eyes. Then I heard him. My eyes opened only to see the creature devour my best friend. I couldn't stand to watch any longer, so I ran. I wept and wept, I was so distraught that I wasn't looking where I was going. I wasn't looking until I collided with an infectious animal, no longer human...

Emma Burnell (12)
Sherburn High School, Sherburn In Elmet

The Test Subject

The virus was worsening. My heart was pounding, legs were shaking and I couldn't hear myself think. Tension in the room was at its peak. The lab was in major shutdown. We could hear the infected species growling at us, begging for cures. We knew this day would come, punishing humans. Upstairs was unsafe now. We knew we had to make it to the basement. Was it safe? Would we be the last humans to walk the planet? All these questions fluttered around my head. I thought to myself, *the test subject*. I ran. Test Subject A was unaccounted for...

Casey Brewitt (11)
Sherburn High School, Sherburn In Elmet

Failed Experiment

The last drop fell into the test tube. Only ten more minutes and Doctor Brown would be freed from the sterile hell of a lab.

He poured the solution onto the fly, then, with plutonium in hand, attached copper wires to it. He put a cigarette lighter to the flask and electricity shot down the wires.

The fly buzzed to life but only a second later he realised its genetic code was transforming at an alarming rate. Then he felt the bite. He screamed as radiation poison morphed him into a decaying mutant.

By the morning, no one was left...

Bobby McNicholas (13)
Sherburn High School, Sherburn In Elmet

The Truth Of The Mess

The man limped closer. I was frozen solid. "It's okay boy, it's me..." His voice was familiar. Then I placed it. It was Grampa, now torn and splattered with blood. I wanted to trust him, but how? He was trapped in this zombie-ridden suit that I couldn't free him from. Suddenly, we were encircled by more of his kind. Under layers of violence, they looked like they were trying to escape. A few did not. I supposed in the quick second before I was gone, they were the first. I heard a boy's scream and then it became distant.

Matilda Mundy (13)
Sherburn High School, Sherburn In Elmet

The Creatures

The year was 2045, the cure for cancer had been discovered but the side effects were deadly, creating unspeakable beings. Bloodthirsty creatures were roaming around the desolate streets. The human race was in jeopardy. A creature was coming, coming at speed for my friend. I had to watch, but couldn't. She was dead. Blood and corpses were spread over the blood-spattered streets, in them lay my friends and my family, all dead. I had to run far away. A creature grabbed me. I ran for my life, I escaped but I had to leave before I was dead too...

Lucie Ann Conqueror (11)
Sherburn High School, Sherburn In Elmet

My Father

I could not scream, I could not run, I could only hide. My father hunted me. Yet it wasn't really him. It wasn't my dad, it was something awful, something disgusting. My dad was going to kill me, one way or another. The parasite that had taken over his body was making him do this - he would never do this to me. That was what I told myself anyway. Then suddenly, "It's okay boy, it's me." The pain was worse than I'd ever felt before. Slowly, I lost control. Then my body wasn't mine any more. *Grr!*

Timothy Collyer (13)
Sherburn High School, Sherburn In Elmet

It

It had won. It had caught me. They said it was coming and it had. It had broken through our walls and ripped the city apart. Torture was its goal. My insides churned. It spread through me like a bullet from a gun. It had broken into our heaven, our place of sanctuary. Surely no one would survive now? With my body weak, I gazed into the destruction. Into the poisoned world. Into repulsive surroundings. Blood, brains and bones paraded down the streets. Nothing could stop it now. Dilapidated buildings, charcoal-grey clouds. It was the plague...

Callie Moy (11)
Sherburn High School, Sherburn In Elmet

Home Base 1

The last drop fell into his throat. This was going to change the whole world. The virus spread faster and faster, very few survivors lived to tell this deadly tale. I woke up in the dead of night. It was one o'clock. I walked carefully, trying to avoid standing on anyone. Scared, I looked through the cracked, dusty window. I saw a middle-aged man so I thought I might help him, but then I heard him chanting something. He was a brain licker. I rushed downstairs and pulled the siren. I looked outside. It was too late. We were surrounded...

Hayden Stewart (11)
Sherburn High School, Sherburn In Elmet

They Were All There

A cold hand grasped mine. "Run," said its owner. "Run away from it all."

As I ran I saw them coming; all of them. They were just like the green, infected zombies I had read about in books and watched in films but, for some reason, they seemed so unfamiliar. They crowded around her. There was a growl but I saw no more. I didn't watch; I couldn't. They were all coming, I ran.

As I arose from my dark, wet bunker it was all gone; there were no survivors at all. Standing up, I turned. They were all there...

Lauren Underwood (11)

Sherburn High School, Sherburn In Elmet

Stranger School

Something scuttled under my skin... what was it? I saw a bright glow travelling up my arm; the strange creature under my faded, purple skin turned black. I muttered to the girl in front. Nothing! Her bag left wide open. Do I peek in? The Professor rose from his chair; slowly approaching the girl. He stood by her side, bent down to her level and said, "You should be more careful!" He took her bag to the front and placed it in his drawer. I started to feel light-headed. I tried to reach for my bottle but fell to the floor...

Elle Hudson Fox (13)
Sherburn High School, Sherburn In Elmet

I'll Die When Hell Freezes Over

We were all bunched together when I volunteered to check. Stupid really, no one who's ever checked has returned, yet. As I turned back to face the dreaded door, the click of ten locks could be heard in the eerie silence. I opened the door.

A scream was emitting from somewhere and I realised that the blood-curdling shriek was coming from me. There in front of me was a human, at least it used to be. Now its arm was so horribly mutilated you'd have thought it was a balloon animal, maggots could be seen squirming. Help!

Martha Tookey (12)

Sherburn High School, Sherburn In Elmet

Toxic Gas

Planet Earth was engulfed by darkness. The land was as dry as bone. The human race was contaminated with a deadly disease. Gas was descending from the gloomy shadows above, murdering those who took one gasp. It was coming for us. We were stranded. Very few of us were left alive, struggling to find non-toxic air that we needed to survive this apocalypse. Desperately, we were looking for safe sanctuary. The others were gone, I was the last. The sanctuary was in the distance but the toxins were creeping up on me. At least I tried.

Ellie Joyce McLaughlin (11)

Sherburn High School, Sherburn In Elmet

Cure?

A boy named Ben Smith had a very normal life. He was popular and had a lot of friends but only up until he was 13. When he turned 13, a zombie apocalypse broke out. It's been two years and him and his parents had managed to survive it. The whole apocalypse happened when an embalmer was doing illegal and dangerous things. However, a scientist had found a cure they could take as an injection. It would stop them turning and would stop the whole zombie apocalypse. But there was only one problem, his parents were anti-vaxxers!

Abi Lister (12)
Sherburn High School, Sherburn In Elmet

Let's Join Them

The world's now nothing but a host to those... things, and of course, their meals. Crazy to think one party could cause all this chaos. I mean the mindless, ravenous-for-flesh type of chaos. Their eyes, stone cold, only able to seek out death and create it, no remorse, no sense of even knowing what they were doing. The entire planet is in ruin. Only bloodstained walls and endless screaming are evident. It might just be all a dream. I mean, they might just see it as a hazy flash to simply drift off. Soon I will know...

Grace Alexandra Murphy (11)
Sherburn High School, Sherburn In Elmet

The Poisonous Cloud

The giant poisonous cloud rises into the sky, people are screaming, running, trying to get out of its path. I shout at them to get inside as the siren sounds the thirty-minute warning to impact. As the cloud blocks out all light, I decide it's time to lock down my bunker. We sit in silence but soon feel the ground shake. A lion's roar of the cloud hitting us with winds like talons clawing at the door. Luckily, the door holds fast. Time passes slowly, making me nervous. What is happening out there? Can we survive?

Callum Edmondson (12)

Sherburn High School, Sherburn In Elmet

Test Subject A

The infection had spread. It was all my fault. I should never have taken my eyes off him. I should have made sure Test Subject A was secure. Now my monsters were coming for me. Their broken nails, their jagged teeth and their decaying skin. They were coming. I bolted to my house but I knew they were fast. My idea on superhumans didn't go to plan. This was a cataclysmic event. I dashed through the open reinforced door and I saw the cold decaying hand on my shoulder. It was him. My personal demon. Test Subject A...

Isaac Grima (13)
Sherburn High School, Sherburn In Elmet

The Cure

The cure had to be here somewhere. All of the people in Sherburn were infected with a bug, except for two people. So they stuck together and they couldn't leave each other's sight, just in case they got the bug. The old scary doctor had to try and find the medicine to cure the bug before the last two people got it. The doctor had to be careful, just in case he got it too. If he got it, he wouldn't be able to make the medicine to cure everyone else. *Bang, bang!* It was too late! Everyone had died!

Jasmine Wilks (12)
Sherburn High School, Sherburn In Elmet

The Cloud

The giant poisonous cloud rose majestically into the sky. I know I really should not have been playing around with those toxic chemical test tubes. I ran away as fast as my legs could carry me. The yellow cloud started to spread as I rushed back home. I did not think much of it until a couple of minutes later, there was a news report saying that there was a mysterious yellow gas and it may be deadly to humans. My face a ghostly white, as I realised that I had just created the death of the entire human race...

Lucy Bell (12)
Sherburn High School, Sherburn In Elmet

Rainy Day

The giant poisonous cloud rose into the sky in the middle of the night. Then it started to rain and the people started to scream. The rain was burning their skin. They ran into their houses and stayed there for the rest of the night.

The next day, they went into a bunker for a few days. The rain continued. They met a scientist hiding in a house that had been destroyed. He said he could make a cure but he needed raindrops and a flower. He made a potion and threw it into the air. The cloud disappeared.

Charlie Houston

Sherburn High School, Sherburn In Elmet

The Poisonous Bug

There was a peaceful town in the middle of England where everyone was happy. But then a girl found a flower and it had a bug on it. Not just any bug, but a poisonous bug. When someone looks at it, it makes them go insane. The girl looked at it and from that day on, she was never the same. She went around talking to herself like she had people beside her and then the whole town went insane. What they didn't realise was that the bug had possessed her and from that day, the town wasn't the same.

Abigail Lax (12)
Sherburn High School, Sherburn In Elmet

Out Of This World

Caitlin's back from space but is staying in a room and no one's allowed to see her. So tonight I will break in and ask her what she has done?
Later that night I come back, no one is there. I break the door open and as soon as I walk in it feels like I have just breathed in water. Someone has just arrived at the building. I sprint out and shut the door behind me.
The next morning, I decide to go for a walk but everyone around me has dropped dead! I am confused. What is happening?

Georgia Young (12)
Sherburn High School, Sherburn In Elmet

The End

This was the end. It was like I was deaf, blind and senseless. I was the only survivor; the houses, my home, the Hazel City Orphanage, was dust. I was only ten years old, facing the end of the world. I was all alone, everyone I knew was gone. I walked down the desolate street, not knowing where to go, not knowing what to do. My only instinct was to survive but for what purpose if I was the last of the human race? I was filled with horror at the thought that I was the last of my species...

Caitlin Jane Cocking (13)
Sherburn High School, Sherburn In Elmet

The End

So here it began. The human race was falling. People were dying. I just couldn't have it. My leader had told me to keep going but how was I supposed to? My group had slowly died. One by one. As sad as it was, I wasn't one to care. My mother was long gone. She was strong but had to go. Just like all the others. I wanted to go but not to make me or my group suffer. Our lives were in danger, I was the only one that could help us now. Then I heard an ear-splitting scream...

Dorinda Ford (12)

Sherburn High School, Sherburn In Elmet

A Battle Until The End

The dark and stormy night dawned upon me as I heard the moaning of the zombies as they approached my house. I was on the watchtower with my gun. Then I heard a huge clunk which had broken the front door. I quickly ran down to grab my child and wife to bring them upstairs. They were soon making their way to our position. I was shooting all the zombies at the front to try and delay them, but there were too many. I reached into my pocket to get ammo. It was all gone...

Harry Cobain Woodward (12)
Sherburn High School, Sherburn In Elmet

The Mad Scientist

I saw it dashing from one person to another, penetrating anything in its way. Its overcast raven spikes stood up, slicing the remainder of us left. Giant poisonous parasites scrambled around the streets, biting and scratching everything they could. I tried to stop them but they were too powerful. All I could see was its bristles, trying to hurt me. A dark shadow looked at me as I knew he was here to defeat me. I stood up but my arms were heavy, then all went black.

Thomas Bickerdike (11)
Sherburn High School, Sherburn In Elmet

The Death Is Here

One day, I was in my lab working on a special cure and suddenly, everything went silent. Darkness everywhere around me. Nowhere to go, nothing to see. I thought to myself, *I can get through this*. I called my colleague and asked him to get down here quickly.

A couple of minutes later, I was working on my cure when I could feel something moving inside. I was so creeped out, my hands were red and my body was hot as lava. Then I stopped...

Harry Shane
Sherburn High School, Sherburn In Elmet

An Infection Like No Other

The cure has to come from somewhere, I thought. I had spent two years confined to Percy's lab...

The contamination appeared when politicians all met in Pyongyang for the twentieth anniversary of Peace Day. When they travelled back to their homelands, disaster struck. The citizens of Pyongyang turned violent to one another.

Everyone said it was President Trump who did it to get back at North Korea.

The infection of violence spread rapidly around the globe, making everyone ask, "Is there a cure?"

Finally, one chilly Friday evening in Percy's lab, we found it! The solution! Finally, peace was restored.

Paddy Murray (13)
St Augustine's RC School, Scarborough

Fallen Souls

The world had fallen. Great empires, gone, cities destroyed, given way to a disease unleashed by those supposed to protect them. They had come, wolves in sheep's clothing, arms out, shepherds herding sheep. Those that'd answered were... changed. 'Perfected'. Given places among the stars. And those who didn't? They faced the consequences. It all began with poison in the water, death unleashed, and it all ended with a cup pressed to parted lips, cool water spilling onto tongues. The thump of corpses. All throughout, Death waited, her eyes ablaze, excited for the fallen souls that'd soon join her...

Jessica Little (11)
St Augustine's RC School, Scarborough

Asylum

Bang! They all escaped, every last patient of the asylum. The disease was now spreading, spreading through the country, affecting everyone who breathed in the same air as these creatures. Everyone would die.

Two hours later, listening through the glass of the misty windows, Mary heard the noise of the infected hobbling around the street, terrorising those oblivious to what was going on, not knowing they were approaching death.

Mary's hands were shaking, dropping the glass she was using to hear the noises outside whilst she was trying to hide from the creatures in white medical gowns...

Ben Moorhouse (12)
St Augustine's RC School, Scarborough

The End Is Nigh

Bang! A puff of smoke rose into the air.

"The gas, it's ready!" shouted the scientist - but he was terrified as the gas started to affect him! It all went black...

Thousands have died from this poisonous gas, but a group of friends are prepared to find the cure. Scavenging the science lab hastily to look for a cure, they are the only ones who can save the entire human race!

Suddenly, a tube smashes onto the floor.

"I've found it!" declared James.

They leapt into the helicopter, ready to drop the cure. Would they save the human race...?

James Briggs (12)
St Augustine's RC School, Scarborough

Whitby Contamination

Athena and Alex were on a trip to Whitby when a vampire bat bit their pet. Surrounding them were vampire-zombies, trying to bite them, so they joined the apocalypse. All of a sudden, Athena and Alex were in a top-secret base filled with all sorts of gadgets.

"Let's send a signal to a satellite then use the animal scanner to find the cure!" suggested Athena.

1 minute later...

"Albino bats are the cure!" Alex announced.

"I'll use the shape-shifting gloves to turn into an albino bat and you use the zapper bracelet to stun them," said Athena.

June Darlow-Castleton (12)
St Augustine's RC School, Scarborough

The Cure

"Sir, we now have the Zylelon B, we are ready for dispatch," said the voice of his chief assistant with a cold glare in his eye.

Sir nodded with a subtle smile. "Now, go."

Crate by crate, the Zylelon B was taken to every single hospital in the UK. With Sir admiring his evil plan, he realised his dreams of annihilation were fast approaching.

The nurses innocently injected the 'cure' into the patients, not knowing they were spreading a disease with no cure and dispersing it in record time.

One by one, the patients left this world, hurting and crying.

Bailey Orrells (12)
St Augustine's RC School, Scarborough

Last Man Standing

The rash is thumping, pulsing, throbbing. I can feel the parasitic creature inside me. There is no cure. I can feel it scuttling under my skin, eating me from the inside out. Contaminated through food and water, nearly everyone has what I have. Boils have begun to form, sores popping and becoming septic. Multiple sclerosis, my already lifelong condition, getting worse...

We are listening to other family members' screams as people die. The worms inside me are eating and reproducing. It's only a matter of time before my family and I transform into zombies and the apocalypse comes...

Christina Salisbury (12)
St Augustine's RC School, Scarborough

Poisonous Water

You can't touch it; you can't look at it; you can't even sniff it! If you do, you die. It's here now; whatever was all over Russia and Africa had now spread to Europe. The delicious tasting water is killing us and we unfortunately can't do anything about it. Screaming, crying, it's all you can hear! Everyone's horrified at what's coming next. No one's calm! Hiding, frightened, thirsty for it, but no, we can't have it, there were just too many chemicals in it. There are dead bodies everywhere. We need to do something about this or we'll all die...

Sandra Kukurowska (13)
St Augustine's RC School, Scarborough

Contamination Story

The virus is spreading; everyone's breaking out in fevers and getting weaker by the second! I have to work fast, or everyone will be too weak to take the antidote; endangering their lives! An antidote that's been lost for thousands of years. It's said the potion needs five ingredients from 'mythical creatures; except someone spotted one of the 'mythical creatures'. A phoenix, which was said to be as bright as the sun itself! How am I meant to find the ingredients from creatures that are so good at hiding that they are believed to be mythical until fifty years ago?

Sian Nichola McDonald (13)

St Augustine's RC School, Scarborough

Parasite

It has been 203 days since the first person was infected. It was a typical Monday morning, it was rush hour in the subway and the train came like a bullet, a powerful wind behind it.

As the wind weaved through the crowds, people fell in waves. Some people were still standing. Moments later, they rose, mutated and disfigured. They attacked the immune. They were usually children and the elderly. The screams echoed in the tunnels and some escaped the massacre. Blood and green pus spilled out of the corrosion in their heads. Viciously, they started attacking their vulnerable victims...

William George Baniqued-Smith (13)
St Augustine's RC School, Scarborough

Vine Touch

There was my sister, shaking uncontrollably, vines almost bursting through her skin.

"It's okay, Tia. I'll find the cure. Promise!"

She tried to hold me, but I jerked away. I darted down the streets, trying to find any clue to where the antidote was. I saw the bodies dispersed along every corner.

It was hopeless. There was no way of finding it. It could be anywhere in the world. I turned the corner and, suddenly, my skin pricked as I felt the brush of a plant stroke my skin.

I was infected. I started to shake. I drifted into oblivion...

Emily Elizabeth Owen (13)
St Augustine's RC School, Scarborough

Doom

5th of April, 2059. 100 people died and it was my fault. It was a terrible idea. Innocent people disappeared at the drop of a tear. Obviously, those people were strangers to me, 100 humans gone 'for the rights of mankind'. Like killing people will save us from the world crumbling right beneath our feet. We could wipe out the entire human race. The government will release the gas tomorrow. They're just power-hungry, vile - argh! Curse my science skills! If I didn't find that mysterious liquid, the world wouldn't end! I had one thing to do to stop this...

Maia Jarmany (12)
St Augustine's RC School, Scarborough

The Last Hour

I'm in a cold cardboard box. All alone, got nothing to do but write this down. I've started having old person sensations: weak, powerless, can barely move. It started when young children started dying. The world was puzzled. More people died. Everyone started wearing hazmat suits, the poor had nothing. I'm one of those people. People have now got private bunkers, we have nothing. When people were infected, they were killed. But we, the nice ones, put them in cardboard boxes, they get to decide if they want to die. Here I am, in a cardboard box, deciding...

Alec Randall (12)
St Augustine's RC School, Scarborough

Chemical Vortex

A strong perfume filled the air. The winds from the tornado had become slower. I looked around at everything that lay lifeless and damaged. Stepping out from under the splintered table, I moved to what was left of the front of our house. Shock surged through me as my eyes met the sight. People, lying helplessly, taken by the destructive winds.

Scents whooshed over the few remaining people and as they breathed in the poisonous air, they dropped to the ground. Why hadn't this happened to me? Questions raced through my mind. Who was going to save me now?

Ella Mai Brown (13)
St Augustine's RC School, Scarborough

Poison Invasion

Poison was beginning to invade easily as Halloween was coming around. Transfigurations were being made everywhere. The world was turning out to be run by zombies! Would I be able to retain my mind after the attack?
Shadows appeared in front of our domicile. I just hoped that it wouldn't be the time my life had to expire. A loud, deafening knock rocked the entire house. The silhouette of an ill-favoured person was stood outside of the house. This was my established death. Would I now be the one to perish first, or would I be the one to survive...?

Misty Byju
St Augustine's RC School, Scarborough

The Cure For Cancer

"That's it! That's the cure for the horrific illness Grandma has; all I have to do is dial the number and it will be on my front doorstep in seven days." Little did I know, in the lab, another contaminated substance was mixed with the water accidentally. This meant whoever consumes it, dies...
Once arrived, it was rushed straight to Grandma. She sipped the bottle all day to the point where there was not a drop in sight. She said she started to feel better already, but little did she know, she only had six hours to live...

Sienna Leigh Cunningham (13)
St Augustine's RC School, Scarborough

The Fatal Mistake

A terrible thing has happened. The government have made a huge mistake. A fatal mistake...
You see, the government had a new prevention for brain cancer. Everybody took it except for my family. Now people are changing, mutating into zombies. We are now running, running from my best friend Charlotte. She has been mutated.
I can taste the blood in my mouth from biting my tongue and I can smell the smoke from the fire the zombies have started. My dad is shouting me; my little brother is crying. I know how to stop this, but I need some help...

Molly Faith Squire (12)

St Augustine's RC School, Scarborough

A Horrible Trip

It was the worst trip ever! Basically, we were on our way to paradise. We got warned at the border that we had to travel during the night because the sun was deadly. But we insisted that we wouldn't go in the sun. Next minute, we were on the tropical beach (in the sun!) at least they were. I wasn't. When we got back to the hotel, nothing happened, they were perfectly fine. The morning was something different, their skin was dry, their vision was going and their stomachs were killing.
A month passed, they still haven't found a cure.

Chiela Robertson (13)
St Augustine's RC School, Scarborough

Toxic

Let me recap, toxic chemicals were spilt into the lake. Animals then got mutated and were able to infect humans. Humans got a disease from the chemical, they weren't able to recover, then died a horrible, painful death. Now, I am stuck in the safehouse, wild animals at the shielded doors. No contact with any other humans. All animals on Earth have the chemicals in them. My heart drops, a single fly. It flies past me but in reality, it is unbelievably slow. It is getting closer, too close. Then, the inevitable happens and the human race is gone.

Louis Eastwood (13)
St Augustine's RC School, Scarborough

Disastrous Disease

I was awoken by a thump.

"What was that?" I yelled with a ton of terror in my voice.

Smash! It must've come from downstairs. I waited, my pillow ready for combat...

The slight sound of scuttling feet filled me with dread. Suddenly, out of nowhere, the door creaked open, its green eyes staring into mine. Swiftly, without any hesitation, I struck it with my pillow. It howled in pain, then proceeded to stumble out of the window and crush the neighbour's car underneath it. It progressed into the darkness...

George Dickinson (12)
St Augustine's RC School, Scarborough

The Asteroid

Why? Why? It's all the asteroid's fault. The human race has been contaminated. 15% of the population has gone. I always have nightmares of me being contaminated. I can see deadly skulls lying around. My heart is beating rapidly. Why did the asteroid come here in the first place? Every day, I see an innocent human asking us to open the dome, but we can't. Every night, I pray, asking God for this to be over - but it never happens. In the dome, we have to be silent. One piece of noise and it's over. What will happen next...?

Albin Johnbosco (12)
St Augustine's RC School, Scarborough

Turning Tides

21st June, 1941: the disease is still spreading. It is said to be a parasite, a disease that sticks to you. The war is still raging on; the Axis and Allied forces have joined up to fight it.

At home, people have had it worse. There's nothing to protect us. We stick in groups. We will either kill them all or wait for the seasons to take their toll. We haven't been told there is no cure yet. All we know is that it infects the brain.

France, 1941; it's spreading through our boys. We can't hold on much longer...

Frank Denham (12)
St Augustine's RC School, Scarborough

The Plague

A breakout of the plague last occurring in 1924-1925 has made its return, infecting over half of the city already. If you're reading this, please do the following: 1. Don't let anyone in or out of your house. 2. Do not open any letters after this one. 3. If you see any form of rodent, do not interact with it.

Our scientists are working hard to clear the poison that's been identified. We hope for this to be over soon. If you have any ideas, please ring the police as the government has now been wiped out by the plague.

Lola Cammish (12)

St Augustine's RC School, Scarborough

Creepy Chaos

Halloween. The best time of the year for me. My sister told me, "Artie, let's try the plane this year." I stood still. I was shocked. The helicopter was bad enough. The island (Halloween Scares) is the best. Once I was on the plane, I noticed a guy in the corner of my eye. He kept looking around. Out of nowhere, he took out a syringe and stabbed the person next to him. He died immediately. I sat staring. He didn't stop there. He turned towards me. I ran to the toilet. I would be safe in there, wouldn't I?

Lucy Webster (11)
St Augustine's RC School, Scarborough

Gone

My rash had spread all over my body. I was dying and my time was running out. With every step I took, I could feel myself getting weaker, my eyesight blurring and fading away. I was stranded in the lifeless city - hopeless.

Slowly, I lost all control of my body, starting from my legs, working its way up to my head. I fell down on the concrete road like a sack of potatoes.

I lay there for hours in unbelievable pain until everyone drifted away. The world was gone in an instant, as if it was never actually there. Gone...

Oskar Zoremba (13)
St Augustine's RC School, Scarborough

Scream

I stood there in shock as I looked at the population scale, it was going down quickly! The disease was going to be coming to us soon. We had to find a cure. Time was running out. The disease was getting closer every second. I could hear people crying in despair. I thought, *why? Why did they let the venomous spider loose? Why? Just why?* I kept asking myself over and over again. Suddenly, I heard screams. Not a child's scream, an adult's scream. Then I heard banging at the door, which creaked. Then silence...

Amelia Cooper (11)
St Augustine's RC School, Scarborough

Russians' Bombs

There's a planet called Earth. On Earth, there's one country that has high-tech gear that can send bombs infected with a virus to every other country. You will then get an illness and turn into a zombie. The Russians will only get the illness if they're bitten. The only way to get a cure the Russians say is to cut off a part of your body. The Russians have guns to shoot the zombies if they get too close, but it takes a whole gun mag to kill 10 zombies. What will happen if the Russians can't control them?

P Jay Flanagan (12)
St Augustine's RC School, Scarborough

The Glowing Fly

Doctor Larry hid under the table. After the big explosion, he stood up to find a big hole in the ground with green inside it. He snuck towards the crater to find the fly that he did the experiment on flying across the room whilst glowing green! It flew out of the window and Doctor Larry thought nothing of it, so he left.

The next day, he looked at the television and he saw that a fly was infecting millions of people and killing them! Doctor Larry knew exactly what had happened and he realised what he had done...

Finlay Earnshaw (11)
St Augustine's RC School, Scarborough

Spider Bite

I'm here now, at the party. I'm just about to get some food and a spider bites me. I walk upstairs and get very dizzy. I can't see. I fall to the ground. I pass out on the floor for about 30 minutes and, when I wake, there's a doctor checking me over. He says that there's no cure to make me better. I go home and wash the area that was bitten with antiseptic.

When I wake up, it's all green and has pus coming out of it. It's going to be like this forever because there's no cure!

Rebecca Strickland (12)

St Augustine's RC School, Scarborough

A Day In My Injured Life

Seriously injured, I soldier on. Broken, the majority of my bones in my body splinter and crack. What should I do? If I'm near someone else, they will injure themselves. It's contagious!
I'm in my house. Nobody can see or come near me. I'm lonely and depressed, stressed and confused. Each day in my life, I wake up lonely and sad, dreading the day ahead. I get ready slowly, as I'm in no rush and, for the rest of the day, I do absolutely nothing. I hope this contagious injury goes...

Isabelle Towse (12)
St Augustine's RC School, Scarborough

The Massacre

Everybody is secured in the dome. Only 5% of the population is stuck outside. Diseases are spreading quick and there is no cure. People are catching the disease even though they are in the dome. No food is left. Nothing is safe to eat or drink. We are running out of oxygen and our skin is turning into a pale blue. No supplies are left in the dome. All we see are the silhouettes of the people outside knocking on the walls for help. Everyone is dying. Please help! I've tried everything I can. I am praying...

Bhavana Binooj (12)
St Augustine's RC School, Scarborough

Laser Tag

The sun has made a disease. A disease that all started off on a normal summer's day. When suddenly it turned dark, lightning, thunder and rain... The crowd started to spread out and hide. The rain had now been going on for about 30 minutes and there was nobody in sight. But then, unexpectedly, the sun started to come back out again and everybody came back out. The sun started reflecting off stuff and lasering the crowd, making them fall to the ground. What had gone wrong? Nobody knew. Were they next? Run!

Molly Murray (11)
St Augustine's RC School, Scarborough

Zombies

The last drop falls into the test tube. I either go out and die or stay in and die? I don't have enough time to decide. The time's ticking away. What should I decide? The zombies need a medicine to make them better. It's now or never. I need to get the medicine. I've found some antibiotics. Will that help? I'm not sure it will help! To get it into them, I need a syringe to stab them with to help them come back to life. Will this help. Could we live with this or not? Will we all survive?

Archie Colin Austin (11)
St Augustine's RC School, Scarborough

Lost Week

It had been a good holiday in Johannesburg. We were on our way home but I wasn't feeling very good. I was feeling sick. So when I got back home, I visited the local doctor and they were shocked. They asked where I had been for the last week. They told me I had Ebola. After they told me I remember passing out. When I woke, I remembered the red and black spider that had bitten me. I was holding it at the airport I loved spiders, but not anymore. I was never going back there again.

Josh Beecroft (12)
St Augustine's RC School, Scarborough

Spiders

Recently, there have been mutated spiders escaping Oak Ridge Laboratory. A contagious virus that gets passed on by being touched by the spider is spreading. The human race is at risk. There is no cure, the spiders are giving birth rapidly and there is no way of stopping them except for with a giant spider, infused with uranium. The only place with uranium is the FG (Federal Government) but they are 35 miles away. There is no time to waste. The whole world is in our hands!

Corey Ormston (12)
St Augustine's RC School, Scarborough

The Secret

The secret federal council is setting a bomb off to destroy the world. There is only one person that can cure everyone. He is Dr Strange. He's the only one that can stop the destruction and stop the council, once and for all. They're trying to get rid of the world, so they can create another. Dr Strange has been working on the cure. He has only been able to make a small amount, enough for one person. He is trying to make more. The bomb has just dropped...

Kaiden Sleightholm (12)
St Augustine's RC School, Scarborough

Come To Papa

Brian worked late on the Necronce Virus. He had one more substance to transfer into the container. As the last droplet splashed in, Brian barely had time to think before an ominous, purple mushroom cloud formed. It made its way to Brian and before he could react, it had tricked him and disappeared into his mouth. Brian choked and was knocked out. Within seconds he was back, tense and cold and he thought to himself, *who am I? What am I? Although I am not certain, I know I'm hungry for flesh.*
"Come to Papa, I won't bite... too much."

Jamie Holdich (13)
The Read School, Drax

Infection

I ran frantically, hoping I'd make it in time. I burst into my bedroom, flattening the door and flinging my toys across the room. After I grabbed all the blankets, I ran to the living room trying to prepare myself for the horror I was about to witness. Nothing could have prepared me for that... Nothing! The infection took each member of my family one by one. It started with a cough and ended in immense pain and a rotting body. The infection doesn't kill, pain does.
It's spread and killed like a Mexican wave. Is hope forever lost?

Millie O'Brien (12)
The Read School, Drax

The Thing

Through my bedroom window, I can see people dropping like rocks. The 'Thing' is coming towards me; it's scaly, green and yellow with blood dripping everywhere.

Then, all of a sudden, I hear the opening and closing of the front door, footsteps are coming along the hallway. Then I hear the creaking of the stairs. I dive under my bed trying to be as silent as I can. My bedroom door opens and an awful smell enters the room. The breaths are getting louder, my heart quickens. The gnarled feet appear in front of me. I close my dark eyes...

Verity Haigh
The Read School, Drax

Zombie Cat

As I walked through the toxic Tower of London, I could smell the damp on the walls of the spooky corridor. I thought I could hear footsteps coming from behind me. I turned and there in front of me was the shadow of a zombie cat! Suddenly it pounced at my leg. I instinctively ran for my life in fear of being infected. I stumbled into a rotten door and everything went black.

As my eyes adjusted to the darkness, I could make out a message on the wall which appeared to be written in blood: 'Escape or die'.

Camran Cook (11)
The Read School, Drax

The Day Time Remembered

Shivering in my freezing cold lab, I had been studying so hard in here to find a way to stop this new miniature creature becoming extinct. It was black and had shiny scales along its back.
The cure had to be in here somewhere!

The creature crept carefully towards me. It looked appealingly into my eyes as I checked my test tubes to see what I could find. There was nothing there I could use to save it. Whatever could I do before it was too late? The poor little creature was slowly getting much weaker...

Sally Featherstone (12)
The Read School, Drax

The Rash In Wensleydale

The rash was spreading, pulsing, hurting. All over my body was a red rash. I noticed half my village had it and it was spreading fast.

"What is happening? It's itchy," said Jerry.

Trying to get doctors, people waited in pain. News spread that a dirty man was about and spreading his germs. Things got scary, people were dying.

"I want to run away, it's getting worse, why is nobody helping? Do they want us to die?"

"Don't panic, they are trying their best," said Rachel.

"Breaking News - Locals in a village in Wensleydale are getting smaller! Stay safe!"

Brodie Allinson
The Wensleydale School, Leyburn

Fatal Fever

The cure had to be here somewhere. Three scientists almost perfected the cure to this deadly disease, the one that engulfed almost the entire world before it snatched them up too, it must be here somewhere...!

Here! My heart was pounding in my chest as I opened the envelope labelled: 'Cure. Do not open'. I was about to save the human race. I slowly opened the folded paper... "It's unfinished," I whispered to myself, tears brimming in my eyes. I was left with no choice, I would need help. I had to find the last humans left on the planet...

Chloe Cumpstone

The Wensleydale School, Leyburn

Run

The rash is spreading, pulsing, hurting. I have to keep running, they can't know who I am. My focus is blurring, I need to keep strong for him.

The serum they injected is oozing like death. The experiments are unpredictable and have made mutations and abnormalities. I wonder what I will become? A flesh-eating zombie or a bloodthirsty beast that shifts on a full moon?

The more fortunate grow wings and can fly away but some become the forsaken, who forget who they are and attack everyone they see.

I keep running and I see a figure. It's him...

Poppy Hainsworth (13)
The Wensleydale School, Leyburn

SCP Containment Breach

"SCP 713 and SCP 091 are unaccounted for," boomed Doctor Jerry over the speakers. "All D-class personnel please remain in your quarters, Nine Tail Fox is entering the SCP laboratory to re-contain SCP 713 (aka the plague doctor) and escort the scientists out of the building. Avoid SCP 091's chambers, its doors are malfunctioning and if you see SCP 091 don't break the line of sight from it because it may seem like a statue. But, if no one is looking at it and you blink, SCP 091 will snap your neck at the base of your skull."

Connor Rosbotham
The Wensleydale School, Leyburn

Practical Gone Wrong

The last drop fell into the test tube. The blue acid turned into a cloudy liquid. We heated it up on a bunsen burner until it boiled, and I mean boiled. Most of it evaporated and there was not much left. Then, suddenly, the tube cracked and thirty seconds later, *bang!* It went up like a rocket and the chemical was airborne. The acid cloud covered the ceiling and dropped to the floor. Everyone panicked and wondered what to do. Mr Tree started choking and fell to the floor. We were all dropping like flies. How would we survive?

Callum Fowler
The Wensleydale School, Leyburn

One In A Thousand

The rash was spreading, pulsing, hurting everyone in its sight. It wasn't your everyday illness - a plague so deadly yet hidden.
Fourteen years have passed and there's still no cure. A bad experiment ruined the world. Unfortunately, the ratio of people to grots (as we call them) is one to a thousand. It's time for the heroes to show up and the villains to lose. We have no plan, no hope. What we have most is something to fight for. Our aim is to rebuild the world, make it a better place. We need a miracle, quick!

Maciej Nuprejczyk (13)

The Wensleydale School, Leyburn

Contamination

The rash was spreading, pulsing and itching as they took a sample of my bubbling rash. The scientist was all suited up. A pinch of my skin fell into the tube which started to bubble and turn green. The bubbles were too much for the tube. *Bang!* The test tube exploded, the glass flew.
A small, harmless-looking fly entered the room as the scientists evacuated, it got closer. It landed but I didn't think anything of it. I looked down at my arm, I was in pain and my arm was gushing blood. I dropped to the floor...

Luke Dent

The Wensleydale School, Leyburn

Contamination

I finally emerge from my cold underground home, my arms, legs and feet numb. I'm going towards the direction my dad gave me and hopefully won't get bitten or scratched by the walking creatures. Now I've packed my food and water in my backpack and a large hunting knife in my sleeve. The map is saying to go north, so I look at the moss on the trees and walk that way. I'm looking for a place to rest before dawn when they come out to kill.

I have found a fallen tree where I can rest, hopefully...

Lucas McCulloch
The Wensleydale School, Leyburn

Contamination

We finally emerged from our underground bunker. Our rations had run out and we were starving. 2152 was when we were banned from going outside due to an airborne virus caused by a science experiment gone wrong.

Gas mask in hand, I poked my head out, looking for the green fog that meant death. No sight of it, I stepped out and started to scavenge what I could find. I tripped, pain shot up my leg. I sprained it as well as launching my mask out of reach. Then I saw it - creeping over the horizon - the green fog...

Cleo Baker
The Wensleydale School, Leyburn

Something Scuttled Under My Skin

Something scuttled under my skin, I could feel it scratching and coursing through my veins. It would only be a matter of minutes before it covered my whole body. I started to have thoughts... Could this be a good thing or a bad thing?

A few days later my life is changed, I am a new man. It has changed me into a superhero, I am changing the world with my power. Saving people, holding up buildings, my body is surging with power, it's a great feeling and all this has come from one insect within my body.

Aidan James Simpson (13)

The Wensleydale School, Leyburn

Toxic

Test subject A is unaccounted for. No one knew where it was. We started to search, the lights went out, the only light was coming from a flickering Bunsen burner.

Suddenly, the flame jumped and started a fire that quickly spread. It burned down a shelf which had a test tube with the letter A on it. It dropped to the floor and let out a toxic gas, killing everyone in the room. The gas leaked out of the room into the building and the fire was non-stop. Nearly everyone was dead only a few people escaped.

Riley Teasdale
The Wensleydale School, Leyburn

Contamination

The cure had to be somewhere. The thumping of the door irritated my ears. He was moaning and I knew at that point I didn't have much time. I looked in his eyes as they started to close. I was praying. The knocks were making me delusional. I realised I was going to die either way. Then I found it. But it was too late, he had changed like the rest of them. I cowered in the corner, knowing I was going to die. He pounced on me with a scratch, then I had changed too.

Lucy Smith

The Wensleydale School, Leyburn

The Biggest Earth Contamination

It exploded! Run! The highly dangerous experiment went wrong. If people inhale this, they'll die! Plants have gone...

Call everyone, we need help, one million people are dead, humanity is in danger, we can't live on Earth. People have two minutes of oxygen, this experiment is taking it. With no oxygen or water, the Earth is going to disappear. We only have one option... Die!

This contamination's getting worse, we are the only people alive, but it is coming to us and we have no place to go.

The contamination is here, we're nowhere safe, I've something to say... "Bye."

Sofia Pemartin Carrillo (12)
Upper Wharfedale School, Threshfield

Everyone's Dead

The voices were getting louder. An eerie scream in my head. "It's only in my head," I repeated to myself.

People dying, or rather, people killing themselves. I wasn't paying attention anymore, only thinking about the voices, I had no one. Numb from the pain, somehow the voices getting to me.

I heard this crash, then blood, silently sneaking through the crack in the door. Probably another one dead, everyone had the voices, not just me. I couldn't cope anymore. "Stay strong," I repeated over and over again. "It's all in my head," I said. "Everyone's dead, what about me?"

Aine Kelly (13)
Upper Wharfedale School, Threshfield

The Last Hope

Earth was now a desolate wasteland. No animal other than human remained. All across the globe; barren ground.

There was a small resistance - the last of our kind. They were trying to survive.

The last shelter; the only hope. You choose the forbidden name, it lay just south of where Deutschland or Germany used to be. The Zeye were coming.

'"Forster... no!" Blood spattered. "No, help, no!" the voice died out, Elaine saw only black.

In the vault, the final, only survivor sat quivering.

"Elaine... Forster?"

Bang! No, the whole world infected, ended gone... gone...

Teddy Cook (13)
Upper Wharfedale School, Threshfield

Menacing Malaria

Spewing, retching, snorting, malaria was spreading rapidly, reproducing faster than lightning over the infected world.

"Ouch!" Every step I take, every breath I breathe hurts like hell. *Gurgle*, my throat tingles and stings. *Blah*, I puke again. I would have to go to the hospital but I've got no money, no house, no family. Sick, I live on the streets.

I see a man in a white coat trudging towards me. Maybe he's curing me, maybe he's getting rid of me. *Blackout!*

I find myself lying on a hospital bed coughing up blood. Have they cured me? I hope so.

Elliot Ashley (12)
Upper Wharfedale School, Threshfield

John's Mistake

"No. Yes. No." Dr Frank tried helplessly to find something that could defeat this virus. If he'd never tried to find a cure for the common cold this wouldn't have happened. This virus killed within twenty-four hours, but with great pain. "Goodness! Please save me!"

Within minutes of being infected by the virus he was on the floor, dying in pain. Frank took some sulphuric acid off the side, downed the whole bottle and curled up in a ball, preparing to die.

In the morning he opened his eyes, expecting to be in the afterlife.

"The cure has been found!"

Bradley Peter Smith (13)
Upper Wharfedale School, Threshfield

A Little Mistake Of Mine

What have I done? I was just helping humanity wasn't I? Humans, once civilised creatures and me, Dr Khazak, helping them, not turning them into prowling monsters. The serum I injected into a small amount of the population was meant to be resistant to all diseases. They are alive, but not as they were. Prowling, deadly monsters, ripped and shredded, misshaped, courtesy of me.

The serum's effects spread across the world. No one knew why. Any time I walked outside onto the lab balcony I heard a cacophony of howls, growls and screams from down below.

I'm the only human...

Lucas Shutt (12)
Upper Wharfedale School, Threshfield

Manipulation

The rash was spreading, pulsing, hurting. I heard the screams of children as they cried for help. The rain's been infected for years. Jackson and Layla watched their parents die in front of their eyes as the rain came down on them. Jackson now had responsibility for Layla.

They travelled to their aunt's, avoiding the rain and the infected with glowing purple eyes.

A mile before their aunt's, a dog crept around with glowing eyes and manipulated Layla's mind, showing her mother. Layla fell for the trick.

Jackson tried to stop her, she slipped his grip. The dog lunged...

Abbie Marshall (15)
Upper Wharfedale School, Threshfield

Zombie Attack

Running, panting, "Argh!" the camera spins out of my hand. I pick it up and start running again. I see something shiny on the ground. "Aha, a gun!" I take it to blast the hearts out of zombies.

I run over to the nearest gun shop, find bullets, guns, BLTs and water. I look around. "Help!" I have a camera, I start to talk, telling people where I am, trying to broadcast. I feel alone.

As I start walking someone says, "Hey," shining a bright light. "I got your message."

I run to their car to go somewhere safer.

"Yay!"

Zack Daniels (12)

Upper Wharfedale School, Threshfield

Water Contamination

It's been three months since the accident. You can't touch the water, otherwise you slip into a deep coma. We can't find the right filtration system. Only a hundred people remain, but we still have over 10,000 combinations. There's no point, but for some stupid reason we keep going.

My best friend Sammy drank the water today. She fell to the ground almost immediately. Now I'm alone, nobody to turn to; no family, no nothing but a few people. Most can't speak my language and some are just children waiting for their parents to wake up from their everlasting slumber.

Jessica Jane Ferridge (13)
Upper Wharfedale School, Threshfield

Death Of The Species

The rash was spreading, pulsing, hurting. The bed was warm, I was warm, I tried restraining the vigorous shaking. People around me shaking, coughing, waiting. My coffin waiting. Nobody to cure it, everyone is infected. The few survivors were in protective suits and they came round checking for heartbeat and turning off monitors.
The cold, wet gloves touch my neck, checking my pulse. He looked at his watch and left.
Two weeks later the hospital was almost empty. Just me and two others infected. No person in a protective suit. It was my time, my body shook and... Blackout.

Charlie Bond (14)
Upper Wharfedale School, Threshfield

Ice Cream Madness

The best ice cream is being sold this summer. It's phenomenal! The most popular ice cream is the pineapple chocolate by Izzy's Incredible Ice Creams. It's so popular it has almost run out. But the doctors are finding some unrecognisable symptoms that have never been seen before. They include vomiting and hiccups. The doctors are finding no cures. 97% of the world's population are dead due to lack of hospitals and doctors. The world is dying rapidly! If someone doesn't do something, the world will end, the entire human race is going to be wiped out! What should I do?

Samantha Cole (13)
Upper Wharfedale School, Threshfield

Human

They were following me. I could see shadows behind me. The whole of my species had come alive. Freakishly alive.

I ran from them, my family with me. "Stop!" Running, running, our short legs ran as fast as we could. Doctors screaming at us to stop. We didn't listen to them, we kept running but they caught us. "Stop!" Needles in their hands, millions of others crowded together, scared! People being injected all around me. A violent murder scene. I was infected, my porcelain face still as ever. My owner holding me, pretending I was a human, still human!

Izzy Willis (13)

Upper Wharfedale School, Threshfield

Implant

I'd been watching them with cameras and they hadn't blinked. They'd been turned into automatons with the technology I'd created. I knew I'd have to act like them; I couldn't hide in the bunker much longer.

I opened the door. Crawling out, I gazed around hyper-cautiously. I was sure nobody was around. I crept through the dark. A light flickered behind me - and another - until there were a myriad dots and I knew instantly what it was. The light in the chip! I couldn't run. Before I knew it they implanted the chip that wiped out humanity into my neck...

Zoë Holme (14)
Upper Wharfedale School, Threshfield

The AI

Humans were close to none, the AI, it ruined us, crippled us, made us the slaves. We were powerless when they attacked. They took control of our money, our cameras, our phones... everything.

We had become so reliant on technology to do everything! They were in our heads, our minds. They controlled our every move. We tried revolting, we tried everything, they knew we were coming, they knew every time. How?

Dr Dorkins made them powerful, smart. We tried shutting them down, their code was unbreakable, inscrutable.

You had one shot at breaking it, if not - you were dead!

Kai Asquith (13)
Upper Wharfedale School, Threshfield

Who Killed Mr Barns?

After ARIA, the new security AI was created, the toxin doors were opened. A huge disaster happened.

The accident took all the lab's resources and, three days later, Mr Barns died mysteriously. But it was too late, the disaster spread, not only across the lab but across the country. The air was polluted and poisonous. Everyone was emigrating, trying to escape before it was too late and the disaster took over the whole world.

Some scientists have tried to blame ARIA for the disaster, but we couldn't find any signs of it. The real question is - who killed Mr Barns?

Álvaro Pemartín (11)
Upper Wharfedale School, Threshfield

They Called It The Invasion

It was mysterious, the mutation they had created threatened them all. The pale beige flesh-covered monster began to tread towards them at a menacing pace. The restaurant fell silent (not that anyone could understand them anyway).

The man behind this terror was Grange, just Grange.

They started to turn them into blood, flesh and bones. No one knew what or why it had happened, but one thing that they inevitably understood was that there was no way back and the end wasn't near.

More and more of the planet was being invaded by their scientific name - homo-sapiens.

Peter Johnston (13)
Upper Wharfedale School, Threshfield

Dark, Darker, Yet Darker

They did it. It's all their fault. They tried to get rid of the rest of the world but in the process... doomed us all. The bomb, it turned us into brittle husks, most of humanity died instantly. I'm barely hanging on anyway. We need to make ourselves powerful again and that requires sacrifice. One soul... Only one soul remains, collected from dead, broken souls. I need to extract its power, its determination to live on.

The extractor is near completion, the bomb radiation side effects have helped my new abilities. I, Dr W D Gaster, will save us all.

Oscar Gamble (13)
Upper Wharfedale School, Threshfield

The Burning Candle

I was one of the many who'd already caught the deadly, spreading disease. My whole body covered in the agonising, oozing patches. I'd been held in isolation, locked away from the world, from my family, solitary. Darkness surrounded me filling me with depressing thoughts.

I was soon to die out, just like the dim, glowing candle in the corner of the room. The flame flickered vigorously, I flinched with excruciating pain. Everything was slipping away, pain seared inside me. The candle continued to flicker, then it stopped, just like that, the candle burned out.

Chloe Evans (13)
Upper Wharfedale School, Threshfield

How I Met My Nightmare

I was trapped, no way out! Then... I started to cry, not tears but blood! This wasn't normal. I was crying blood. I tried my best to escape, but there was no hope. I was in a single room, no doors, no windows, no escape!

Suddenly it got cold... deadly cold. How was this possible? There was nothing in this deadly space, but one old ripped blanket. I could see something, mist... thick mist. Where was it coming from? It was surrounding me. I fell to the floor.

"I'm your worst nightmare!" growled the spirit. "Now die."

Alicia Heseltine (14)
Upper Wharfedale School, Threshfield

What Happened Next?

The giant, poisonous cloud rose into the sky from the factory near Cadbury's.

The smoke alarm had gone off. A huge ball of gas rose into the air, then a plane flew over and the oil and the gas mixed...

Something happened.

The next thing, *bang!* Now everyone went into a panic. People couldn't see or breathe and from what I can remember a few people went blind. People ran into water for protection and some stayed in shelters. Most of them were flushed away by the water. There were only a few survivors living in trees and holes.

Jessie Allen (11)
Upper Wharfedale School, Threshfield

Feral Again

I am running, running from a Feral. My small legs can't keep up with the speed of my thoughts. The Feral lunges forward, sinking its teeth into the bare skin of my neck.

My name is Lucy Ryder, I'm eleven years old. My thoughts are beginning to wander to the wrong things, Feral things. If only my parents could get back with the cure. If only I could live to save the human race. But I can't. I'm dying.

I'm trying to imagine home again until I hear the gunshots. Everything goes dark.

"Feral down!" says Officer 342.

Paige Spriggs (14)
Upper Wharfedale School, Threshfield

Cold Blood

Blood dripped like water dripping on a rusty, old drainpipe. Everyone was dead. If I didn't get out soon I would be just like the others. I could feel the agonising pain under my skin. The bitterness of the cold ached my head. Something or someone had torn a hole in my leg. It was swollen and becoming infected. I could barely breathe. I could feel my lungs collapsing on my bones. I would die soon, without surgery I couldn't last much longer.
Eerie screams prompt my soul, my skull rattled in the wind. I blacked out, beaten and bloodied...

Ailish Kelly (13)
Upper Wharfedale School, Threshfield

Poison

2205.

We are trying to make a new breed of human.
Experiment 102 has failed, all our attempts have failed. Commence experiment 103. System warning, critical!
The lights went out and I panicked as something came walking towards me. What had I created? Most life on Earth has been eliminated. Our goals were bold. What were we thinking? A new breed of human? I laughed at the stupid thought of creating an upper life form. I unsheathed my knife and prepared for the worst. I tensed up and out of the blue I was attacked, goodbye world.

Daniel Berry
Upper Wharfedale School, Threshfield

Suicide Missile

The white sky is what we call it, the flash was instantaneous as the sky was filled with a blinding, maleficent, harsh light that you physically couldn't bear to look at. The world was peaceful, one of the most peaceful times in history. Well, that's what we all heard on the news and thought.

This was days before the suicide missile was launched from the centre of Asia. The news was all over it. Authorities were all claiming an accidental launch of the new type of nuclear missile. We knew this would destroy humanity with drastic effects...

Harrison Donne (13)
Upper Wharfedale School, Threshfield

The Changes In The Globe

After the mad dash, we all sat watching, waiting, agonising over what would happen next. An hour went by, no one had said anything, not a ripple of movement had been made. No one wanted to say anything, why would they? What was to say now? You're probably wondering by now what it was. Well, it's global warming. It was easy to blame other people for this, the politicians, scientists, but really it was us, we caused this, we made it happen and now we have the toxic seas, freak weather and wildfires devastating our homes. Now we are dying.

Isabella Sacks Alderson (13)
Upper Wharfedale School, Threshfield

That Bite

That bite doesn't look like a bite, it looks... infected.
Every day more people are turning into complete
freaks. They look normal, not like any zombie
creature. Nearly the whole population is infected.
I'm safe, I'm in a secret bunker, but with ten of us
food is getting low.

The world is dead. Broken windows and fires. I try
to listen but there's nothing, just silence.

Bang! The bunker door closes. I try to open it
again. I turn round, I am surrounded by them. I am
screaming and shouting, everything goes black...

Jorja Woollaston (13)

Upper Wharfedale School, Threshfield

Bitten

Crunching twigs shattered in the blistering heat which beamed on my thin neck. His deep voice echoed on the vast Sahara. I took cover in a shady tree. Dry as a bone, the branch collapsed to the dusty floor, clouds of rubble drifted amongst tumbleweed. Clumsily, a clattering engine roamed on unknown roads. A herd of people stumbled out. The instructor led the bunch towards the head of a giraffe. I planned to feed on that tonight. My scrawny legs landed on a short child. An ear-splitting screech went past his ear. A sudden itching as I fled. Bitten!

Sam Meldon (12)
Upper Wharfedale School, Threshfield

Unbreakable

I could feel the poison in me. When would it have an end? The touch of my hands able to kill a dear life. They're shooting - shooting through me, not realising that I'm unbreakable, that I can't be killed. Not realising that the blood on my lips is their blood, that their blood is delicious, that I was designed to kill, to eat human flesh. Only being able to stay alive until they realise that I'm not theirs. That I'm deadly to every man.
Every inch of me wants pressing, deadly revenge. They made me their enemy; a monster!

Felicia Stenzel (11)
Upper Wharfedale School, Threshfield

A Chance?

If only I hadn't started it, I should have known that adding the Berkelium to a cold cell would create bacteria so harmful that plants, animals and fish would be affected. Now only humans survive. My colleague is on life support. I can't bring myself to turn it off.

I am still trying to find a solution, I'm on my last few chemicals. If I look out the window I see bodies littering the gutters. It makes me desperate.

I mix together seven random chemicals. I inject them into my colleague, his eyes flash open... A chance?

Noah Peace (12)
Upper Wharfedale School, Threshfield

No Safe Space

I was coursing through the streets, the pandemic had been released. Nowhere was safe as the Path to the Light had been used. The sun was setting as the danger was rising. As I scuttled, I heard the sound of feasting, the screaming ceased. As the person's last breath had left his bloodied, jagged mouth, arms torn and bitten, they spotted me as their next meal. I bolted, climbing onto the roof, leaping building to building until I wasn't being chased. I saw destruction, cars and houses in embers of flames.
Then it happened...

Korey Michael Hopson (13)
Upper Wharfedale School, Threshfield

The Monsters Strike

There has been a nuclear war that has wiped out three-quarters of the world's population. A lot of people have been turned into monsters. Soon there will be no people left.

People are trying to stop it, it has taken ten years, but people have not found a cure. Scientists have been working hard but most of them had been turned into monsters. A lot of people have not been sleeping to try and find something to stop the monsters. Most of the scientists have been working very hard.

There was only one more problem, it was too late!

Cameron Marsden (12)
Upper Wharfedale School, Threshfield

The Takeover Of Vampires

One bat, one bite is all it took and one dead body. First, my friend, then my family. The bat flew in through the window and bit them on the neck. Blood poured out faster than the water from the tap. I tried everything, I gave them antibiotics, they wouldn't even eat any food.

Days went past, more victims were infected. Nothing helped. My sister said she could smell something, but I couldn't. She smelled blood and tried biting me. I killed them, I tried in the heart first then in the head, I think they're dead.

Amirah Jahangir (15)
Upper Wharfedale School, Threshfield

No Dandruff Mission

It's back here. The white flakes of skin piling into the people's hair. Don't worry Mr Shampoo, No Dandruff Man, is back! He's piling on.
People are scratching their hair out, the contamination is defeating the human race. It's taking over the world. There must be a cure for it. Oh yes, it's back in Tesco. It's 'Mr No Dandruff Shampoo Man'. No one is buying it, so Mr No Dandruff will have to do the job himself.
Then it happens, the world is cured, there's no more dandruff, woo hoo!

Sabiha Ayub (12)
Upper Wharfedale School, Threshfield

Silent

We emerged from the bunker, all bashed, bruised, cut, scared and hungry. The city in the distance was rubble, the buildings in ruins. The trees were tall, reaching the sky. The light dappled through the branches leaking onto the rocky paths. It was silent, we couldn't make a sound. If we did something bad would happen. This thing had killed mankind, we were the only ones left.

We were all walking, skipping over the crisp leaves, dodging the loose rocks... Until *crunch!* She was gone and we were next...

Thomas Knight (13)
Upper Wharfedale School, Threshfield

The New Black Death

It has finally happened. The zombies have come, but they came from some crazy scientist that made the new Black Death. There was no way of stopping it and you return as a flesh-hungry monster with guts like jam.

It has been a year. People have been ripped apart and people that could not take this cruel world have ended it, committing suicide.

The group of survivors that are left are not affected by the Black Death, but they can be infected by the monsters.

They found a boat; they never see land again. Or do they?

Gethin Kerswell (15)
Upper Wharfedale School, Threshfield

The Last Of Humanity

We finally emerge from the underground bunker. Not a single soul to be seen. The sun was shining, the birds were singing. A shiver ran down my spine, my palms sweating, my blood ice-cold. The fear was intense. I had to watch my back for fear of being captured.

I say *we*, but not for long. My dishevelled, broken sister hadn't a care in the world, she was shaking. It was hard to say that we were the last piece of an originally fulfilled art. This was the end of civilisation. Our home turned into a ghost town.

Ruby Winthrop (13)
Upper Wharfedale School, Threshfield

The Giant, Poisonous Cloud

The giant, poisonous cloud rose into the sky as visitors were going to fight. The visitors used a weapon to kill all of the human race. Some thought that it was a normal cloud but others heard that it was a toxic cloud. People visited the shops and some folk stayed inside.

Victims came back, when they'd woken they looked like burn victims with black eyes. I was really scared, I ran into someone's house to get out of the toxic cloud. Luckily, I survived but the other people died. I'd tried to help them...

Mollie Roberts (15)
Upper Wharfedale School, Threshfield

Smog And Lies

We saw ourselves as change, changing control, order and life itself. Our success could only show purpose. We didn't kill those people, they fell astray. We left them lying in disgrace, scattered like parasites. We only assisted those who asked us. We freed those who couldn't free themselves. I personally didn't watch our revelation, all I know is I'm here and I'm Death. I did what no one else could, I lived when no one else would. I survived and that's why I'm standing here above death.

Harry Clifford Gaskell (16)
Upper Wharfedale School, Threshfield

The Curse

We finally emerged from the underground bunker to see the plume of gas rise to the heavens. Only twelve of us remain, the rest gone, forever. Could we survive? Will we survive?

It's been five weeks since it started, how many more weeks will it last? One? Two? More? If we are going to make it through, then we must make a sacrifice. Who to choose? If the gods have cursed us then it's our only option. We have no other choice. It will be a painful death, much worse than before, but more lives will be saved...

Harry Peace (14)

Upper Wharfedale School, Threshfield

The Infected Pills

Hello everyone and welcome to the 8am news. Today's news is about what we believe has been a murder... Our famed Dr Izzy died at 4:30 this morning. All that was left in Dr Izzy's lab was a computer, blood and some pills.

Next morning...

Hello everyone, we are back with the 8am news. There has been another murder, Grace our news presenter. We believe that Dr Izzy gave her patient some pills that carried some type of chemical. This has started a zombie war.

Whatever you do, run fast now!

Chloe Maimee Barbour (11)

Upper Wharfedale School, Threshfield

The Rise Of The Heat

We emerged from the underground bunker, the sky blood-red. We didn't know if we were the only ones left, the heat had killed our neighbours. Our supplies could only last us another week. We needed to find more, and fast. We headed to an abandoned shop, bodies laid in cars, we got everything that we could. I heard a crash behind me, I looked back to see my friend had collapsed on the floor from the heat. I knew I could not help her and we needed to get to safety. I grabbed my sister's hand and we ran.

Emma Falshaw (13)
Upper Wharfedale School, Threshfield

The Ending Of Humanity!

The pestilence is spreading. The world is transforming! Every green-skinned human is lurking for their prey. Mr Smith is running everywhere searching for his lost family. He is desperate for rest.

Months later, the supply of food, medicines, antibiotics is lacking. No antidote works. The last sliver of hope drops when Mr Smith glances down to see his growling parents staggering around the streets. Kneeling down, he decides to join the dead and his tragic family.

The ending of humanity is imminent.

Charlie Smith (14)
Upper Wharfedale School, Threshfield

The Man Who Tried To Save The World...

The school smells of corpses. All the wounded are being carted away by the shipload. The dreadful disease has cleared out 150 born-and-bred students.

I didn't want this to happen, I was just trying to create a new superfood. Something to save the world not to kill it.

The bacteria spread and the killing started. All of those people, those poor, innocent families. I couldn't handle the filthy guilt.

It's me, the ghost of Steve who tried to save the world but killed it!

Archie Allen (13)

Upper Wharfedale School, Threshfield

A Madman

A madman that's what he was. A madman. Cancer was at an end. Disease was at an end. A new race of killers had begun. They came from nowhere, just appeared.

Each country was devastated by one. Dictated, more like killed. If a leader died, then the country died with them.

Then the country became barren... barren! Their demise was met like frozen fire. Africa gone, Asia gone, America gone, only Europe was left. He had created this, but no one would stop it.

Armageddon had begun.

James Neill (13)

Upper Wharfedale School, Threshfield

The Cure

Ten days later, it spread. Everyone contaminated because of me, my work, my experiments. All I wanted to do was find a cure for a disease. It was not my fault that the rat escaped. Who knew it would do this much harm to humankind. Stupid me, what did I make, what did I do?
The door swung open, it was a young woman, she was very pale green with a veiny body and red, glowing eyes. She suddenly twitched, lunging at me, knocking down the test tubes from the table. The cure, it was gone!

Jan Kucia (13)
Upper Wharfedale School, Threshfield

The Last Survivors

One day it was all peaceful, then it changed. There were weird-faced creeps coming at me and one of them ate my friends. I think they were zombies. Two weeks later, there are outposts all over the place, but they are not very strong. People keep dying and I think we are next. Things keep falling from the sky, one of them hit my other friend's outpost but he somehow made it to our outpost. I really miss Mum. I am going to die, I am going to miss this world so badly. Bye-bye.

Alfie Roddis
Upper Wharfedale School, Threshfield

The Boy Who Died By Water

One day, there was a young child, just living normal day-to-day life. He went to go and get a glass of water, but when he turned on the tap the water didn't look as it should have. He took a glass of it to his room. When he drank some he started to feel rather queasy. Things were starting to get a bit hazy. He didn't know what was going on. He began to get scared, everything seemed darker, more like death. He felt his heart beating as he gradually started to fall and die.

Isabelle Lynam (14)
Upper Wharfedale School, Threshfield

Dreams Of The Lost Lands

Khat jolted awake to Matt being ripped limb from limb by one lost soul and she knew he was gone. She sprang to her feet and took off down an alleyway. Suddenly alarms started ringing and she looked out of a window and saw the power plant screaming in pain. The lost souls Matt was trying to stop had powered on the reactor.
She dropped to her knees and began praying as the blinding flash consumed her...

David Elgie (14)

Upper Wharfedale School, Threshfield

 Young**Writers**® Est. 1991

YOUNG WRITERS
INFORMATION

We hope you have enjoyed reading this book – and that you will continue to in the coming years.

If you're a young writer who enjoys reading and creative writing, or the parent of an enthusiastic poet or story writer, do visit our website **www.youngwriters.co.uk**. Here you will find free competitions, workshops and games, as well as recommended reads, a poetry glossary and our blog.

If you would like to order further copies of this book, or any of our other titles, then please give us a call or order via your online account.

Young Writers
Remus House
Coltsfoot Drive
Peterborough
PE2 9BF
(01733) 890066
info@youngwriters.co.uk

Join in the conversation!

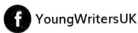 YoungWritersUK    @YoungWritersCW